Just then, Maisy c████████████████████████e

thick coat of tight white curls, long floppy
ears, a soft black nose, enormous jet-black
eyes and a crazily waggy tail. His pink
tongue was hanging out of his mouth and
Maisy was quite sure that he was smiling –
hopefully at her. She wanted to run over and
give him a giant hug and pet his lovely soft
fur. But something was holding her back. She
grabbed Mum's hand. She was nervous. She
wanted everything to work out so much. But
what if it didn't? What if Bruno set off her
allergies and asthma just like all the other
dogs she'd even so much as looked at did? So
far it all seemed too good to be true. Maisy
was convinced that something was going to
go wrong.

"Don't worry, love," said Mum gently. "It's
OK, you can go to him."

www.randomhousechildrens.co.uk

www.battersea.org.uk

Have you read all these books in the
Battersea Dogs & Cats Home series?

BRUNO'S
story

by
Alice Corrie

Illustrated by Artful Doodlers
Puzzle illustrations by Jason Chapman

RED FOX

BATTERSEA DOGS & CATS HOME: BRUNO'S STORY
A RED FOX BOOK 978 1 849 41579 8

First published in Great Britain by Red Fox,
an imprint of Random House Children's Publishers UK
A Random House Group Company

This edition published 2012

1 3 5 7 9 10 8 6 4 2

The Random House Group Limited supports the Forest Stewardship Council
(FSC®), the leading international forest certification organization. Our books
carrying the FSC label are printed on FSC®-certified paper. FSC is the only
forest certification scheme endorsed by the leading environmental
organizations, including Greenpeace. Our paper procurement policy can be
found at www.randomhouse.co.uk/environment.

MIX
Paper from
responsible sources
FSC® C016897

Set in 13/20 Stone Informal

Red Fox Books are published by Random House Publishers UK,
61–63 Uxbridge Road, London W5 5SA

www.**randomhousechildrens**.co.uk
www.**totallyrandombooks**.co.uk
www.**randomhouse**.co.uk

Addresses for companies within The Random House Group Limited
can be found at: www.randomhouse.co.uk/offices.htm

THE RANDOM HOUSE GROUP Limited Reg. No. 954009

A CIP catalogue record for this book is available from the British Library.

Printed and bound in Great Britain by
CPI Group (UK) Ltd, Croydon, CR0 4YY

Turn to page 91 for lots
of information on
Battersea Dogs & Cats Home,
plus some cool activities!

❧ ❧ ❧ ❧

Meet the stars of the Battersea Dogs & Cats Home series to date . . .

Bailey

Chester

Misty

Max

Daisy

Rusty

Snowy

Huey

Stella

Angel

Alfie

Cosmo

Coco

Buddy and Holly

Petal

Suzy

Bertie

Jessie

Bruno

Oscar

The Summer Holidays Begin

The summer term seemed to have gone on forever. Maisy had been longing for the holidays to arrive. And finally, they were here. The last day of term was over. She was free! Well, for six weeks anyway. It was going to be brilliant.

Her best friend, Tessa, who she had been friends with since before she could remember, and who went to a different school, had come over for tea. It was the perfect start to a perfect summer. Mum had bought all their favourite food and laid it out picnic-style in the garden. Maisy couldn't wait to get stuck in and start planning all the cool things she and Tessa would do together over the holidays.

"I'm so excited about going to Spain!" announced Tessa as she picked up a crisp and started delicately nibbling it. "I've never even been on a plane before."

Maisy's heart lurched. This was the first she had heard about Tessa going anywhere.

"Wow!" Maisy replied, trying not to let the surprise and hurt show in her voice. "When are you going?"

"This Sunday," Tessa replied. "Mum got a really good late deal so we're going for three whole weeks – Mum, Dad, Evie and me. It's going to be amazing."

"Oh," said Maisy flatly, her heart sinking and her dreams of spending the holidays hanging out with Tessa shattered. "That's the day after tomorrow."

"I know. How cool is that? And I've got loads of packing to do still," said Tessa  breathlessly, not noticing Maisy's change in mood. "Mum has bought me a gorgeous swimming costume. It's white with pink roses on it, and it has pink straps and little pink bows by the legs. I've got a matching sun hat and beach dress too. She's going to take Evie and me shopping tomorrow in town for all the other stuff we're going to need, like sun cream and new summer clothes and shoes. I really want to get some sunglasses just like yours. I wish you were coming."

"Me too," sighed Maisy, as she imagined the next three weeks without her best friend and how bored she was going to be.

And then Tessa told her about the kids' club at the resort. It sounded incredible. Tessa would be able to go sailing, cycling, snorkelling, water ski-ing and loads of other brilliant things.

Maisy was green with envy and sick with disappointment, although she tried not to show it. It wasn't Tessa's fault, and Tessa had every right to be excited. It was her first ever holiday abroad. But for Maisy the summer holidays that she had

been looking forward to for so long were
going to be rubbish without her best
friend to share them. She was quite sure
of it.

Life is So Unfair!

The rest of the afternoon flew by in a flash. Maisy was determined to make the most of the time she had with her best friend and not be miserable. When Tessa's mum arrived in a huge fluster, Maisy had a little spark of hope that maybe something had happened and Mrs Thompson had had to cancel their holiday and Tessa wouldn't be going after all.

Maisy knew it was selfish, as Tessa and her family were so excited, but deep down it was exactly what she wanted to happen.

"It's a nightmare! I just don't know what we're going to do," said Tessa's mum as she plonked herself down at the kitchen table where Maisy's mum had just placed a cup of tea for her.

Mrs Thompson was looking very red in the face and as if she might burst into tears at any minute.

"What's happened, Mum?" asked Tessa, the worry streaked across her face.

"It's Grandad . . ." her mum began.

"Is he OK?" Tessa interrupted. "What's happened to him?"

A smile crossed Mrs Thompson's face.

"Hold your horses. Of course he's OK, sweetheart. If you'd just have a little patience, I'll tell you what's going on."

Tessa's mum explained that she had arranged for Tessa's grandad to house-sit and look after their big black Labrador, Reg,

while they were on
holiday, but that
he had just had a
call to say that
his brother was
ill in hospital.
"Grandad has
had to go up north
to take care of Great
Uncle Peter," explained Tessa's mum.
"There's no one else to look after him
since Great Aunt Edie died last year, so
Grandad has to go, Tess."

"But what are we going to do, Mum?"
Tessa wailed.

"To be honest, love, I don't know,"
replied Mrs Thompson matter-of-factly.
"It's very short notice to sort something
else out, and if we cancel the holiday
we'll still have to pay for it."

Five minutes ago this would have been music to Maisy's ears. There really was a chance that Tessa and her family would have to cancel their holiday. That would mean having Tessa to play with and no boredom at all – just lovely long summer holidays with her best friend. But when she looked over at Tessa's crumpled face and saw how upset she was, Maisy couldn't believe how selfish she had been; Tessa was her friend, after all.

Maisy took a deep breath.

"We could look after Reg while you're away," she blurted out without really thinking. "He could come and stay here, couldn't he, Mum?"

Mum shot Maisy one of her 'looks'. Maisy's heart sank.

"Maisy, sweetheart, you know we can't do that," said Mum as gently as she could.

"Oh, pleeeaaaase, Mum," begged Maisy. "I'll be super careful, I promise."

Maisy's mum looked over at Mrs Thompson and Tessa and then back to Maisy.

"I wish I could say yes. I would love to be able to help out but we just can't do it, I'm afraid. Maisy, it's one thing you going over to Tessa's to play and quite another having Reg to stay for three whole weeks. Even if he is in another room or in the garden, you're badly allergic to dogs, darling, and will get very wheezy," her mum explained. "If he was here, your asthma could get really bad and you might even end up in hospital again."

Deep down, Maisy knew that her mum was right, and she definitely didn't want to go to hospital again. It was really scary last time and she had missed home like mad. But she wasn't ready to give up yet. She loved dogs. It was so unfair that she would never be able to have one.

"Couldn't he just stay at Tessa's house and we could go round to feed him and stuff?" suggested Maisy.

"Oh, Maisy, that's a really good idea, thank you for offering, but I don't think Reg would be terribly happy," replied Mrs Thompson.

"He'd get very lonely all on his own most of the time. He needs people to play with and a decent walk every day."

"But, Mum, what are we going to do?" asked Tessa with a wobbly voice, her dreams of an amazing holiday slipping away. "Please don't say we can't go."

"We'll have to think of something else," said Mrs Thompson. "I'll ring the kennels as soon as we get home and just hope they can squeeze him in at such short notice."

And with that, Mrs Thompson announced that it was time for them to leave. She thanked Maisy and her mum for trying to help and for having Tessa to tea. Maisy and Tessa gave each other a giant hug.

"Just in case we do find a space for Reg, I'll say goodbye now. Hopefully see you in three weeks," called Tessa as she walked out to her mum's car. "I'll buy you a present, I promise."

All Maisy could manage was a wave and an attempt at a smile.

Things Look Up!

Maisy walked back in from the drive after waving Tessa off, shuffled over to the sofa and threw herself down on it. She didn't even turn the TV on. She just didn't feel like doing anything.

Mum walked over and stroked Maisy's hair. Maisy wriggled away.

"Oh, love, I know you're going to miss Tessa if they do find a place for Reg at the

kennels, but it's not
the end of the
world," she
soothed. "It is
only for three
weeks. I've
taken time off
over the
summer so we
can go on lots
of outings.
You'll hardly
even notice
she's gone."

"That's not it,
Mum," Maisy replied
miserably. "Well, not all of it, anyway."

"If you don't tell me what's up, then I
can't help, sweetheart," Mum said gently.

And with that, Maisy burst into tears

and explained to her mum how she was feeling.

"I love dogs so much, Mum," she sobbed. "It's just totally unfair that I'm allergic to them. Why me? Why do I have to have stupid asthma and get all red and itchy and teary and wheezy every time I so much as even look at a dog? I want a pet so badly – and not a boring goldfish like the school one I borrowed last summer. Freddie the fish was rubbish. All he did was swim around the bowl, open and close his mouth and do poos.

And cleaning out the bowl was disgusting."

"You're absolutely right, Maisy. It's not fair. Your granny was exactly the same, so you can blame her if you like," said Mum, trying to lighten the mood. "But then she did quite like keeping fish!"

It didn't help. Maisy was in a grump and nothing short of magic was going to get her out of it. Maisy's mum was going to need to work some sort of miracle if she wanted to avoid the summer holidays being a complete disaster. And then she remembered something . . .

"Maisy, I've had a thought," said Mum carefully, not wanting to get her daughter's hopes up too much. "I was watching something on TV the other night while you were doing your homework, and it was all about someone just like you."

"What, you mean someone with nothing to do and no one to play with all holidays?" Maisy replied grumpily.

"No, grumble-guts! I mean someone who is allergic to dogs!" Maisy's mum explained.

"So what?" Maisy replied sulkily. "Just because other people are allergic to dogs, it doesn't make me feel any better."

"Well, if you'd let me finish, then you'd find out that this might actually make you feel better," sighed Mum.

She went on to explain that in the programme they mentioned that some breeds of dog can make good pets for people with allergies because they are not as likely to trigger reactions as some other breeds. The presenter, who was a vet, said that this was because

although these breeds are mainly fluffy, their fur doesn't shed as much as other dogs and it is the shedding fur that causes a lot of the problems.

"One of the breeds was a poodle, I think," said Maisy's mum. "You like them, don't you?"

Maisy looked up at her mum, already feeling bad for being so grumpy when all she was trying to do was make her feel better. Her heart was beating really fast. Maybe there was some hope, after all.

"Can we get one? Pleeeeaaase, Mum?" asked Maisy, her misery completely forgotten. "I promise I'd look after it and train it and walk it and everything. Pleeeeaaase?"

"Of course you can, darling," smiled
Mum. "I didn't bring it up to tease you!
Now that you're eight I think you can
handle all the responsibility that comes
with having a pet, and I know how mad
about dogs you are. Plus it would stop
you whingeing to me about how bored
you are at weekends and during the
holidays, so it's a gift to myself really!
And I thought we should try Battersea
Dogs & Cats Home first. Have you
heard of them? They are a
rescue centre

for lost or abandoned dogs and cats, so we'll really be helping a puppy in need. I have already called up and registered with them."

They both laughed. Maisy leaped off the sofa and gave her mum a giant hug.

This was the happiest day of her life. She never thought in her wildest dreams that she would ever have her very own dog because of her allergies and her asthma. Maybe these would turn out to be awesome summer holidays after all.

Going to See a Lady About a Dog

Maisy hardly slept a wink that night. She couldn't stop thinking about what Mum had said. She was going to get a dog. Something she had never believed could happen.

She woke up just as the sun was rising. It was ridiculously early and she knew that Mum wouldn't be up for ages, so she decided to go online and find out everything she could about poodles.

An hour or so later, Maisy heard the radio being switched on downstairs and Mum banging about in the kitchen. She bounded down the stairs, two at a time, desperate to find out when they were going to go get her a dog.

Mum was on the phone. Maisy walked into the kitchen as quietly as her excitement would let her, but she wasn't feeling quiet. She was so happy. She felt bouncy and fluttery inside and she was 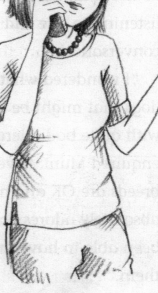 longing to tell Mum all she had discovered about poodles.

"Hello, is that Battersea Dogs & Cats Home?" Mum said into the receiver.

Maisy's tummy flipped. It was really happening! Mum was already on the case with finding her a dog.

She couldn't eat a thing so she sat down at the table and waited as patiently as she could for Mum to finish, while listening to one end of the phone conversation.

"I wondered whether you had any dogs that might be suitable for someone with quite bad allergies and asthma," enquired Mum. "I've heard that some breeds are OK and my daughter absolutely adores dogs but has never been able to have much to do with them."

There was a pause
while Mum listened
to the person on the
other end of the
phone. Maisy crossed
everything she could
possibly cross.
Fingers, toes, legs,
arms. She held her
breath and wished.
She waited for what
seemed like an age.

And then,
finally, Mum
turned to Maisy,
smiled and gave
her the thumbs
up, then carried
on speaking
into the phone.

Maisy leaped up like an excitable puppy and did a celebratory dance around the kitchen, a huge grin plastered across her face.

"Come on then, love. Eat some breakfast and then get dressed," said Mum with a grin when she finally got off the phone. "We're off to see a lady about a dog, and we mustn't be late!"

Maisy could hardly believe it. She had never imagined that it would all happen so quickly. It was hard to take in.

She wolfed down some cereal, hardly tasting it even though it was the yummy chocolaty one that Mum always let her have during the holidays as a special treat. Then she raced up to her room and flung on the first clothes that she pulled out of her wardrobe. She brushed her teeth and hair, washed her face and was waiting for Mum in the hall before she had even finished her cup of tea. Mum had never seen Maisy get ready so fast.

"If only you'd do that on school days," she laughed as she grabbed her bag, keys and the sat nav and opened the front door for Maisy.

As they drove through the sunny morning streets, which were pretty empty now that it was the school holidays, Maisy's mum explained how everything worked at Battersea Dogs & Cats Home.

She told Maisy that although they would meet the dog today, they wouldn't be able to take it home until someone from the Home had asked them lots of questions and come round to look at their house to make sure it was suitable for a dog.

Maisy understood. Although she would have loved to take a dog home right

away, she had waited her whole life to get one, and a few more days wouldn't hurt her.

When Mum had finished explaining the process, Maisy chatted excitedly about the things she would do with her dog and the places they would go, and how she was never going to be bored ever again.

Meeting Bruno

They drove over Chelsea Bridge and
when Maisy caught sight of the famous
towers of Battersea Power Station she
knew that they were almost there. Her
heart was banging in her chest and she
was worried that the sheer excitement
would trigger an asthma attack. It had
happened before . . .

The sat nav directed them to a nearby

street where they knew they would be able to park. They got out, locked the car and walked the short distance to Battersea Dogs & Cats Home.

Mum told the receptionist that they were there and then came to sit down with Maisy to wait until it was time for their appointment. They didn't have to wait long. A few minutes later, a pretty blonde lady who was about the same age as Maisy's mum called them into her office.

"Hello!" she beamed. "Take a seat. I'm Mandy, one of the rehomers here at Battersea. You must be Maisy."

Maisy smiled shyly and said hello.

"Well, it's nice to meet you," continued Mandy. "I spoke to your mum on the phone earlier today and she told me all about you. And, as I'm sure she's already said, I think you're in luck and that we might have just the dog for you. Shall we go and have a look?"

"Yes, please," said Maisy, unable to hide her excitement and her shyness forgotten. "I think I'm going to burst if I don't see it soon!"

Mandy and Mum laughed.

"For starters," said Mandy with a twinkle in her eye, "this dog is not an 'it'! He's a 'he', and his name is Bruno. I've arranged for him to be brought out to the paddock for you to meet him, as  I'm not sure that a trip to the kennels where all the other dogs are would be very good for your allergies."

As they walked out to the paddock, Mandy told Maisy and her mum a bit more about Bruno. He was a hypoallergenic poodle, which is why she thought he might suit Maisy, and he was found wandering around Battersea Park all alone with no collar and no microchip. She told them that when he was brought in he hadn't been very well. He'd had a bad cold and was very skinny.

"Poor Bruno!" said Maisy, trying to understand how anyone could just abandon an animal.

"He's right as rain now though," Mandy reassured her cheerfully. "He just needed a bit of TLC and a roof over his head, and I know he'll perk up even more once he's got a permanent home."

Just then, Maisy caught sight of an adorable white fluffball of a dog sitting patiently in the paddock with another member of the Battersea Dogs & Cats Home staff. He had a thick coat of tight white curls, long floppy ears, a soft black nose, enormous jet-black eyes and a crazily waggy tail. His pink tongue

was hanging out of his mouth and Maisy
was quite sure that he was smiling –
hopefully at her. She wanted to run over
and give him a giant hug and pet his
lovely soft fur. But something was
holding her back.

She grabbed Mum's hand. She was nervous. She wanted everything to work out so much. But what if it didn't? What if Bruno set off her allergies and asthma just like all the other dogs she'd even so much as looked at did? So far it all seemed too good to be true. Maisy was convinced that something was going to go wrong.

"Don't worry, love," said Mum gently. "It's OK, you can go to him."

Maisy felt breathless as she walked closer to Bruno. Her heart was beating at a hundred miles an hour and her palms were clammy. Was it the beginnings of an asthma attack or was it just nerves? She couldn't tell. She turned back to look at Mum, who smiled encouragingly.

"There's no need to be shy," said Mandy, "he's very friendly and it looks like he's desperate to meet you!"

Maisy needed no more persuading.
She crouched down next to Bruno and
before she knew it he was nuzzling into
her and licking her hands, and she
was stroking his beautiful
wool-like coat. He
was gorgeous!

Her breathlessness had completely gone and been replaced with a feeling of total and utter bliss. Maisy could hardly believe it. Here she was with a dog in her lap, stroking and petting him and even having her palms licked, and she hadn't even sneezed.

"I told you he was friendly, didn't I?" laughed Mandy. "I must warn you that poodles can be a bit of a handful though. They do make the most wonderful pets but they're hard work. You'll need to keep him busy and make sure he gets a lot of exercise, and remember to groom him.

Poodles are full of beans and incredibly intelligent, so they get easily bored, and they're prone to mischief!"

"That sounds exactly like someone else I know," said Mum, winking, as she looked at Maisy.

Maisy, now sitting cross-legged in the paddock with Bruno curled up in her lap, said nothing in reply. She was silently taking it all in and promising to herself that she was going to be the best dog-owner ever. There was no way she would let Bruno down.

Mum grinned. She was thrilled to see

Maisy so happy. "Love at first sight," she said.

"For both of them, I think," replied Mandy, as Bruno reached up and gave Maisy a big slobbery kiss on her cheek.

Life is Paw-fect!

Maisy spent the next few days in a state of high excitement. She read everything she could find on the internet about looking after poodles, and took loads of books out of the library too. When the man from Battersea Dogs & Cats Home came for the home visit Maisy wouldn't leave him alone. She followed him around the house and garden, chattering

constantly about
Bruno and asking
the man all sorts
of questions.
After he left,
Maisy felt
that
familiar
fluttering
feeling in
her tummy.
The one she'd
been getting ever
since Mum told
her that she might
be able to have a dog.
The wait to find out whether Bruno
would be hers was excruciating and
Maisy decided that the only thing for it
was to keep busy.

Two days later, Maisy was dropped off at home by her friend Tara's mum after a trip to the cinema. She was still on tenterhooks about Bruno, and was beginning to worry that it had all been her imagination. She opened the front gate, walked up the garden path and took out her key. But as she turned it in the lock, she heard a strange noise. A sort of scuffling, scratching noise, then a whine and a bark. She felt breathless, just like the day she met Bruno. Before she could open the door, it was opened from the inside by her mum. Maisy was practically knocked over by a bundle of white curly fur with a waggy tail leaping up at her. BRUNO!

"Wow!" squealed Maisy. "He's here at last! I can't believe you kept it a secret, Mum."

"I just wanted it to be a surprise, sweetheart," Mum replied. "Now, come through to the kitchen. You can give him his tea and then show him round his new home."

Maisy didn't need to be told twice. She flung her bag on the chair in the hall and raced through to the kitchen with Bruno at her heels.

When she got there
she saw that Mum
had laid out a
brand-new
water bowl on a
mat; the exact
one Maisy had
seen in the Battersea
shop. And next to that
was the gorgeous spotty dog bed Maisy
had had her eye on. Then she
looked down and saw
that Bruno was
wearing a smart
stripy collar with a
silver tag with the
Battersea logo on
one side and her
name and address
on the other.

On the counter was a matching lead, a pouch of dog food, some dog biscuits and two bowls, each with 'Bruno' written on them.

"Thanks, Mum," beamed Maisy. "You're the best! Well, after Bruno, anyway!"

Mum smiled. It was lovely to see Maisy so happy.

Maisy prepared Bruno's food and put the two bowls next to his water. He wolfed it down greedily, his tag clinking against the side as he ate. Maisy stroked his head, still finding it hard to believe how lucky she was to have him.

"Oh, I almost forgot," said Mum, "there's a postcard from Tessa. It arrived this morning. I've left it on the table for you."

"Thanks, Mum," replied Maisy. "I'll read it later. Can I take Bruno out to play now?"

"Of course you can," laughed Mum, surprised at her daughter's lack of interest in Tessa's card. How things had changed in the last ten days! "I thought you would have been desperate to find out what Tess has been up to."

But Maisy wasn't listening. She was already out in the garden with Bruno and was having an amazing time.

Bruno, the Magic Dog!

It was a week since Bruno had come to live with them but it felt as if he'd been part of the family for ever. Maisy had the whole day planned out. She was going to take Bruno for a long walk in the park with Mum, and then she was going to come home and start trying to teach him a few tricks. She had read in one of the many books she had taken out of the library that because poodles were super clever it was quite easy to teach them to do cool tricks, like shaking hands and playing dead. Some could even be taught to jump through hoops. That was her goal! Maisy was determined to have one perfected by the time Tessa got back from her holiday.

"Sarah rang last night," said Mum in between slurps of tea and mouthfuls of muesli. "Poor thing's broken her leg."

Sarah and Lauren were Mum's best friends.

Maisy didn't know where this was leading so she carried on eating her breakfast and daydreaming about dog tricks while sneakily slipping bits of food to Bruno, who was curled up under the table wagging his tail.

"It's quite a bad break so they're keeping her in hospital for a couple of days," explained Mum. "I said I'd go and see her this morning with Lauren. She needs cheering up."

Maisy's heart sank. Now she knew where this was going. Mum wanted her to come too.

"We won't be there too long, love. Lauren's bringing her daughter Becky along too. Becky's nearly seventeen now – I'm sure she'll have lots to talk about. And you can take Bruno for a walk on the way," said Mum, noticing Maisy's downcast expression.

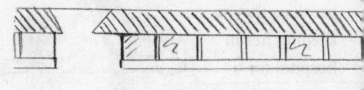

*

An hour later, they all arrived at the
hospital. Bruno was having a whale of a
time, pulling at his lead in his eagerness
to sniff every corner of pavement.
Everything was an exciting new
adventure for him.

"They won't let dogs inside, sweetheart," Mum explained to Maisy. "I won't be long, I promise. You and Bruno wait for me here. Becky will keep an eye on you."

"OK, Mum," replied Maisy, scanning her surroundings and noticing, with delight, that there was a big grassy patch next to the car park. It would be perfect for playing fetch with Bruno. "See you later."

Becky and Maisy wandered over to the grass with Bruno on his lead. While Becky sat down with a book, Maisy pulled a squishy red ball out of her bag. She couldn't believe it was only a week old! It was already very well-loved, covered in bite marks and just a tiny bit stinky. Gorgeous as Bruno was, his breath definitely did NOT smell gorgeous!

He absolutely loved playing, and was getting really good at responding to her commands of 'sit', 'heel', 'drop' and 'fetch'. He was such a clever dog. Maisy thought again how sad it was that his previous owners hadn't wanted him.

Maisy unclipped Bruno's lead and put it in her pocket.

Then she threw the ball. Bruno leaped
after it and brought it back. She threw it
again and again, a tiny bit further each
time. And then she really hurled it – so far
that she couldn't even see it. Whoops!
Before she could stop him, Bruno sprinted
after it, tail wagging, tongue hanging
out and panting like mad.

Maisy set off after him, frantically calling his name and praying that he would stop. She was terrified that he would run out into a busy road.

"Be careful!" Becky called. "Don't go too far!"

Seconds later she caught sight of Bruno, energetically scratching himself against a tree, the ball obviously forgotten. Then she spotted the ball, which had landed in the middle of a hedge. Right next to the hedge was a bench. It looked like she might have only narrowly avoided hitting its occupant, who was a girl of about Maisy's age. She had a bandaged arm and was wearing her dressing gown and she did NOT look happy. Maybe the ball *had* hit her.

Satisfied that Bruno wasn't going to do a runner, Maisy walked over to get the ball.

She smiled at the girl. "I'm really sorry, did the ball hit you?"

"No," replied the girl flatly, tears in her eyes.

"Are you OK?" asked Maisy. "You look like you've been crying. Oh, I'm Maisy, by the way."

"I'm Helen," said the girl. "I'm fine. It's just that seeing you and your dog playing made me feel sad."

Maisy shot Helen a puzzled look.

"I know that sounds really silly," continued Helen, "but it's just completely unfair. All the other patients on the children's ward are having a visit from a dog today as a treat. It's part of a 'pets as therapy' thing. And I really *love* dogs. The trouble is," she sniffed and wiped her nose, "I'm totally allergic to them. They make me really,

really ill. I didn't want to stay in another room and watch the others having fun through the window so I came out here instead."

Then Helen burst into tears.

Maisy smiled.

"I don't know why you're smiling," said Helen in a wounded voice.

"It's just so weird!" laughed Maisy.

Helen sounded exactly like she had at the beginning of the summer holidays. She totally understood what it was like. But before she could explain herself they were interrupted by a loud rustling in the hedge. A second later, Bruno's furry white head popped out, with the ball in his mouth. He looked very pleased with himself indeed. He dropped the ball on the ground in front of the bench, let out a triumphant little bark and padded towards Maisy as if to rest his head on her lap.

The moment Bruno moved forward, Helen shrank back and let out a little yelp.

"It's OK, I promise," Maisy assured her. "I'm just like you. I get really bad asthma and I'm allergic to dogs, well, most dogs, anyway. Bruno is special – that's why I've got him. Look!"

Maisy patted her lap and Bruno leaped up onto it. Then she gave him a huge hug, rubbing her face in his soft woolly fur. "Look, no weepy eyes, no wheezing, no sneezing. Nothing!" Maisy laughed. "Go on, give him a cuddle."

Helen gingerly put out her good arm and stroked Bruno. His fur felt amazing. Just like Maisy, she had never thought, even in her wildest dreams, that she would be able to stroke a dog and not get sick. Her tears were forgotten. She was smiling from ear to ear.

Maisy picked Bruno up and put him on Helen's lap. Helen was in heaven and so was Bruno. He *loved* attention. She gave him a giant hug and he responded by

licking her hand and wagging his tail
like crazy.

"This is so cool!" beamed Helen.
"Thanks. Bruno's a magic dog. I haven't
missed out on the treat after all!"

Read on for lots more . . .

🐾 🐾 🐾 🐾

Battersea Dogs & Cats Home

Battersea Dogs & Cats Home is a charity that aims never to turn away a dog or cat in need of our help. We reunite lost dogs and cats with their owners; when we can't do this, we care for them until new homes can be found for them; and we educate the public about responsible pet ownership. Every year the Home takes in around 9,000 dogs and cats. In addition to the site in southwest London, the Home also has two other centres based at Old Windsor, Berkshire, and Brands Hatch, Kent.

The original site in Holloway

History

The Temporary Home for Lost and Starving Dogs was originally opened in a stable yard in Holloway in 1860 by Mary Tealby after she found a starving puppy in the street. There was no one to look after him, so she took him home and nursed him back to health. She was so worried about the other dogs wandering the streets that she opened the Temporary Home for Lost and Starving Dogs. The Home was established to help to look after them all and find them new owners.

Sadly Mary Tealby died in 1865, aged sixty-four, and little more is known about her, but her good work was continued. In 1871 the Home moved to its present site in Battersea, and was renamed the Dogs' Home Battersea.

Some important dates for the Home:

1883 – Battersea start taking in cats.

1914 – 100 sledge dogs are housed at the Hackbridge site, in preparation for Ernest Shackleton's second Antarctic expedition.

1956 – Queen Elizabeth II becomes patron of the Home.

2004 – Red the Lurcher's night-time antics become world famous when he is caught on camera regularly escaping from his kennel and liberating his canine chums for midnight feasts.

2007 – The BBC broadcast *Animal Rescue Live* from the Home for three weeks from mid-July to early August.

❦ ❦ ❦ BRUNO'S STORY

Amy Watson

Amy Watson has been working at Battersea Dogs & Cats Home for eight years and has been the Home's Education Officer for four years. Amy's role means that she regularly visits schools around Battersea's three sites to teach children how to behave and stay safe around dogs and cats, and all about responsible dog and cat ownership. She also regularly features on the Battersea website – www.battersea.org.uk – giving tips and advice on how to train your dog or cat under the "Fun and Learning" section.

On most school visits Amy can take a dog with her, so she is normally accompanied by her beautiful ex-Battersea dog, Hattie. Hattie has been living with Amy for three years and really enjoys meeting new children and helping Amy with her work.

The process for re-homing a dog or a cat

When a lost dog or cat arrives, Battersea's Lost Dogs & Cats Line works hard to try to find the animal's owners. If, after seven days, they have not been able to reunite them, the search for a new home can begin.

The Home works hard to find caring, permanent new homes for all the lost and unwanted dogs and cats.

Dogs and cats have their own characters and so staff at the Home will spend time getting to know every dog and cat. This helps decide the type of home the dog or cat needs.

There are three stages of the re-homing process at Battersea Dogs & Cats Home. Battersea's re-homing team wants to find you the perfect pet: sometimes this can take a while, so please be patient while we search for your new friend!

1 Register details

2 Match

3 Leaving with your new pet

Have a look at our website:
http://www.battersea.org.uk/dogs/rehoming/index.html for more details!

Jokes

WARNING – you might get serious belly-ache after reading these!

What do you get when you cross a dog with a phone?
A golden receiver!

What is a vampire's favourite dog?
A Bloodhound!

What kind of pets lay around the house?
Car-pets!

What's worse than raining cats and dogs?
Hailing elephants!

What do you call a dog that is a librarian?
A hush-puppy!

What do you get when you cross a mean dog and a computer?
A mega-bite!

Why couldn't the Dalmatian hide from his pal?
Because he was already spotted!

What do you do with a blue Burmese?
Try and cheer it up!

Why did the cat join the Red Cross?
Because she wanted to be a first-aid kit!

What happened to the dog that ate nothing but garlic?
His bark was much worse than his bite!

What do you get if you cross a dog with a Concorde?
A jet-setter!

What do you call a cat that has swallowed a duck?
A duck-filled fatty puss!

Did you hear about the cat that drank five bowls of water?
He set a new lap record!

Did you hear about the cat that swallowed a ball of wool?
She had mittens!

Dos and Don'ts of looking after dogs and cats

Dogs dos and don'ts

DO

- Be gentle and quiet around dogs at all times – treat them how you would like to be treated.
- Have respect for dogs.

DON'T

- Sneak up on a dog – you could scare them.
- Tease a dog – it's not fair.
- Stare at a dog – dogs can find this scary.
- Disturb a dog who is sleeping or eating.

- Assume a dog wants to play with you. Just like you, sometimes they may want to be left alone.
- Approach a dog who is without an owner as you won't know if the dog is friendly or not.

Cats dos and don'ts

DO
- Be gentle and quiet around cats at all times.
- Have respect for cats.
- Let a cat approach you in their own time.

DON'T
- Stare at a cat as they can find this intimidating.

- Tease a cat – it's not fair.
- Disturb a sleeping or eating cat – they may not want attention or to play.
- Assume a cat will always want to play. Like you, sometimes they want to be left alone.

Some fun pet-themed puzzles!

What to think about before getting a dog!

Here is a list of things that you need to think about before getting a dog. See if you can find them in the word search and while you look, think why they might be so important. Only look for words written in black. They can be written backwards, diagonally, forwards, up and down, so look carefully and GOOD LUCK!

SIZE
MALE OR FEMALE
AGE
COAT TYPE
COST
BEHAVIOUR
BASIC TRAINING
HOUSE TRAINING
TIME ALONE
GOOD WITH: PETS, CHILDREN, STRANGERS, DOGS
HOW: ENERGETIC, CUDDLY, STRONG WILLED, INDEPENDENT

Remember: when training a dog, reward works better than punishment.

Can you think of any other things? Write them in the spaces below.

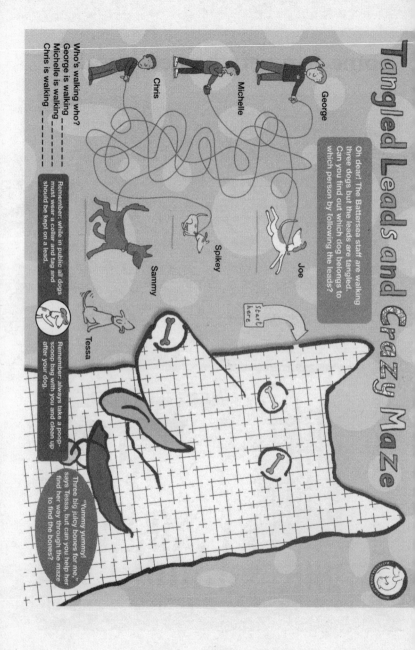

Tangled Leads and Crazy Maze

Oh dear! The Battersea staff are walking three dogs but the leads are tangled. Can you find out which dog belongs to which person by following the leads?

George

Michelle

Chris

Joe

Spikey

Sammy

Tessa

start here

Who's walking who?
George is walking – – – – – – –
Michelle is walking – – – – – –
Chris is walking – – – – – – – –

Remember, while in public all dogs must wear a collar and tag and should be kept on a lead.

Remember: always take a poop-scoop bag with you and clean up after your dog.

"Yummy yummy! Three big juicy bones for me," says Tessa, but can you help her find her way through the maze to find the bones?

Drawing dogs and cats

If you can draw these shapes you can draw a dog:

head ears body tail
neck front legs back legs

Draw your dog in pencil.

Use a pen to smooth the edges and add toes, collar and 'whisker dots.'

Rub out the pencil line.

Add shading/colour.

If you can draw these shapes you can draw a cat:

ears face body front legs back legs tail

Draw your cat in pencil.

Use a pen to smooth the edges and add toes, collar and whiskers.

Rub out the pencil line.

Add shading/colour.

Here is a delicious recipe for you to follow.

Remember to ask an adult to help you.

Cheddar Cheese Dog Cookies

You will need:

227g grated Cheddar cheese

(use at room temperature)

114g margarine

1 egg

1 clove of garlic (crushed)

172g wholewheat flour

30g wheatgerm

1 teaspoon salt

30ml milk

Preheat the oven to 375°F/190°C/gas mark 5.

Cream the cheese and margarine together.

When smooth, add the egg and garlic and mix well. Add the flour, wheatgerm and salt. Mix well until a dough forms. Add the milk and mix again.

Chill the mixture in the fridge for one hour.

Roll the dough onto a floured surface until it is about 4cm thick. Use cookie cutters to cut out shapes.

Bake on an ungreased baking tray for 15–18 minutes.

Cool to room temperature and store in an airtight container in the fridge.

There are lots of fun things on the website, including an online quiz, e-cards, colouring sheets and recipes for making dog and cat treats.

www.battersea.org.uk